OPEN WITH SMILE

AN ANTHOLOGY OF OPEN LETTERS AND POEMS

A UNIT OF FANATIXX

SPECTRUM OF THOUGHTS

AM/56, Basanti Colony, Rourkela 769012, Odisha

A Unit of FANATIXX.

Website: www.fanatixx.in

"OPEN WITH SMILE" by: **Sourav Chatterjee & Priyanka Saraf**

ISBN: 978-93-89106-74-9

FICTION STORIES 1st Edition

Book Formatting: Mayuri Valanju

Cover Design: Sagar Samal

WRITER'S DESK

DISCLAIMER

This anthology is a collection of POEMS, OPEN LETTERS and our editors have made their efforts to edit the work of our co-authors. All the poems have been placed unique in this book.

We have tried our best to check for plagiarism in the write-ups featured in the book. The book consists only the original write-ups.

ACKNOWLEDGEMENT

I would like to show my gratitude to all the wonderful people in my life.

First of all I would like to say thanks to my Best friend, Sayan Chakrabarty, for your support in every phases of my life. Thanks for your support and inspiration! You made me realize the meaning of Friendship! Thanks for understanding me more than anyone, thanks for accepting my real self and motivating me towards the journey of Writing!

Thanks to my Parents for your moral support and your blessings in every step of my life!

Thanks to my elder brother Chayan Chatterjee for your support and helping me in every step of life!

Special thanks to my lovely cousins Mamai, Piu for lovely company, my friend of crime! I just can't describe how much I love you in words...!!

Thanks my loving sister Atasi for all those Craziness, thanks for making me smile!

Thanks to my best friend Prodipta. Thanks for listening my every story and tolerating my angry and mad side! Thanks for those memorable scooty rides! :') Enough! I can't praise more! :-/

My school friends- Shayamsundar, Tanusree, Debarpita, Tamogno, Shubhomoy, Sanjib,thanks for the all beautiful memories!

My best buddies Sandip, Suraj, Subhajit for all the bike rides! And for being with me always!

My friend Sanchaita(Mimi), for making me realize that it doesn't matter how long you know each-other but it's about how to understand someone from the very first day when you meet them.

And thanks to my all online friends for being too good and helping and guiding me for my writing!

Thanks Doctor Nadine Brune for saving my life many times! Thanks for being so humble and supportive!

My Instagram friend- Sara ,for being so friendly and supportive towards my Writing journey! ☺

My Instagram friend Darlina, for always praising my writing skills and always loving my poems! Thanks for the love and support! ☺

Thanks to whole team of FanatiXx Publications, for making my dream into reality!

ABOUT THE EDITOR

Sourav Chatterjee

Sourav is an avid reader, writer, actor, director, nature lover. He is also passionate about photography and film direction.

He is born and brought up in Asansol, West Bengal. His immense love and dedication towards literature has made him what he's today. He was recognised among top 100 authors of India for his book "Rainbow of Thoughts", along with being felicitated with the title "Author of the Year" for the same. He worked in the project of "Future of the Past" (Preservation of Heritage) in Kolkata .He worked internationally as a Communicator and Story teller. He is the author of "Rainbow of Thoughts", "Sprinkling Thoughts". His works in various books such as "Tales from Hearts", "Flames from the Soul" and "Euphoria or words" as a compiler and editor has been recognised worldwide. Apart from all these achievements, his writing has been published in different national and international anthologies.

His hobbies include learning new things, meeting new people along with exploring new places. He is blessed with a selfless heart willing to work for child education.

He holds a diploma degree in Communication from Burdwan University along with a bachelor's degree in Media Science (Hons).

He is currently working in Entertainment Industry and is pursuing his passion as a full time Writer.He can be contacted through:-Mail: souravchatterjee692@gmail.com

Instagram: @souravchatterjee8293

ACKNOWLEDGEMENT

I would like to show my gratitude to all the wonderful people in my life.

First of all I would like to say thanks to my Best friend, Sayan Chakrabarty, for your support in every phases of my life. Thanks for your support and inspiration! You made me realize the meaning of Friendship! Thanks for understanding me more than anyone, thanks for accepting my real self and motivating me towards the journey of Writing!

Thanks to my Parents for your moral support and your blessings in every step of my life!

Thanks to my elder brother Chayan Chatterjee for your support and helping me in every step of life!

Special thanks to my lovely cousins Mamai, Piu for lovely company, my friend of crime! I just can't describe how much I love you in words...!!

Thanks my loving sister Atasi for all those Craziness, thanks for making me smile!

Thanks to my best friend Prodipta. Thanks for listening my every story and tolerating my angry and mad side! Thanks for those memorable scooty rides! :') Enough! I can't praise more! :-/

My school friends- Shayamsundar, Tanusree, Debarpita, Tamogno, Shubhomoy, Sanjib,thanks for the all beautiful memories!

My best buddies Sandip, Suraj, Subhajit for all the bike rides! And for being with me always!

My friend Sanchaita(Mimi), for making me realize that it doesn't matter how long you know each-other but it's about how to understand someone from the very first day when you meet them.

And thanks to my all online friends for being too good and helping and guiding me for my writing!

Thanks Doctor Nadine Brune for saving my life many times! Thanks for being so humble and supportive!

My Instagram friend- Sara ,for being so friendly and supportive towards my Writing journey! ☺

My Instagram friend Darlina, for always praising my writing skills and always loving my poems! Thanks for the love and support! ☺

Thanks to whole team of FanatiXx Publications, for making my dream into reality!

ABOUT THE EDITOR

Priyanka Saraf

Priyanka Sharadchandra Saraf lives in Pune, Maharashtra. She has studied E.N.T.C. Engineering. She loves to pen down her thoughts through poetry. She is the author of the books, "Rainbow of Thoughts" and "Sprinkling Thoughts"

She was recognized as one of the "Top 100 Debut Author" for her book : "Rainbow of Thoughts" Also, she has worked as an editor and compiler for the anthology "Tales from Hearts". Her work has also been published in various anthologies.

She likes to study Indian culture. She is interested in English literature and Indian mythology. She wants to write about social issues. She believes that there is something good in everyone. Working for the betterment of the society is the main motive in her life. She is thankful to her family and friends for all the success in her life.

You can get in touch with her through

email: priyankasaraf021@gmail.com

Instagram: @priyankasaraf021

Wordpress: sarafpriyanka.wordpress.com

Facebook page:
https://www.facebook.com/HEART_Beads-961665737306868/

WRITERS DESK

An Engineer by choice and a writer because of her passion. Alice was born and brought up in Indore, Madhya Pradesh and lives there with her family. Alice always believes in making connection through words. She loathes talking about herself but can be persuaded to do time to time.

You can contact her at alicetinna@gmail.com or on Instagram (_hazel_eyed_girl)

Alice Tinna

MAKING MINE

Turn up love,

It's so cold out there.

Let me have a bite from your side,

And maybe we can move around for a while.

Hold still, your ankle have something,

I should hold you,

And take you to the paradise of our love.

Tonight is the Turing point,

Maybe we can just be a little polite

And more of a furious kind.

I'll taste you and you can have me,

And I'll let you go down with your hands clutching

Then we can go through the love for the first time,

And if it went well we can have this several time.

Just to know, that I have planned something more,

Just a little more energy you need,

Maybe I can give you some.

Go down on your knees

Let's start this.

And remember to have me in

So that you can feel full.

Just another time

We can go with something from my sight.

But for now have me the wildest way you can,

It's your night.

Making mine.

NO LIMITS

No more whispering or closed eyes,

but blindfolded, still .

Touching your lips with mine,

I want to move where it counts.

I want to love you booming,

in Blaze

and in centre of everything.

I want to love you openly

under sun and moon ,

under everything ,

you can feel .

I want to feel you from within,

release back your taste from my lips,

And kiss you passionately

As slow as the longest of days,

Inclouded , unrushedd, pleasant,

In the middle of the spring night.

And if I fail this time,

I want to try again.

I want to set "no limits" to our love.

DYING STAR

I held it close,

So close to me, that it was

really hard to pull it away,

For anyone but you.

I ran from the bunch of flowers,

To stay between the thrones;

This is how I chose you over

many more.

I still remember the last time,

I smiled because of you,

But for now my demons wants

To kill you.

As far as I know,

I am walking on the mud,

Holding it still,

My heart full of love.

Still gripping so hard,

And grasping so strong,

The rope I have kept holding on,

Is now burning so shine,

Like a dying star.

FLY TO ME

Was it easy?

That easy for you to not longing for me?

About my waist and down to it,

Don't feel like touching anything.

And about my eyelashes that once you told make you a little wild?

What about the back kisses and hugs , which you gave me the most?

Don't you miss anything?

They way you take the path from top to bottom,

And again on top.

From the behind and sides,

Don't you miss the mess we created while driving crazy everything around us?

Don't you just feel like giving a long kiss and never separate the lips?

Don't you miss the moan when you give me hickeys?

Was this so easy to forget?

Every night when I come crawling towards you,

When you smile because you know what I want.

And then you stay there and keep me engaged for a while and

then everything you do is nonstop.

Well with this distance now

I know you miss them all.

So let the fire burn without any fuel,

And fly to me keeping no rules.

RESTRAIN

This hurts more than the pain can cause,

I wish I can just dwell deep inside the well and never come back.

This sudden air of sadness,

Keeps me awake.

There lies no sleep underneath

And my heart ache.

I wish I can go on a walk to a place,

From where there is no coming back.

I wish to stay away from all the world's mess.

Maybe to the point of life where I'll again meet happiness,

But for now,

I just want to cut off

And restrain myself.

Anurag Singh

24

Anurag Singh is a poet, writer, and author of the "Bewitched" and "Chronicle of Fear" along with 8 Anthologies. A passionate writer, voracious reader and seeker of love. He is a huge fan of E.L James, J. K. Rowling and Stephanie Meyer. A multi-dimensional person with so many interests and opinions.

Anurag is best known for his Instant Poetry. Visit him at www.anuragwrites.co.in

Instagram : @Anurag300485

Twitter : @anurag_writes

DEVIL

Descend from Sky,

I am tired of all the signs

I am grateful for nature,

I have received a message of new lives.

Listen to me, False face of men born

Whispering and sly, A lot of hives.

Happiness is the world, like wedding golden ring

The particles of emotions are the devil

and I have all the knives.

Every new morning, I am in because I cried at dawn

Break the rules, Rip-off, I am here to rise.

Slogan shout, spread your feather

See what it is all about,

Every morning will be full of rives.

Just kill me and You will win one or the other day

So do not miss the light,

The sun rises in the direction of light

Illuminate your body,

I am the sign of sunburn

I am the hope, I am the devil,

I am really changing all lives.

CHILDHOOD

Let's Today give a knock on the doorstep of childhood

you are going to visit those villages where we live up.

Where you tired of eating and eating

Wherever you look, there was the nature of great beauty

Where the news of the drunkenness, or the thunderbolt

Childhood, childhood, childhood, childhood

When the sun rises, it is a blessing and The childhood was a rising sun

Then there were two letters on all the land and that childhood

They have stolen from the tree and buried in the ground, By searching hidden treasures,

Childhood, childhood, childhood, childhood

The villages had its own charms and childhood was awesome there.

The story of "Gudda Gudiya "has been lost and childhood became a dream

The childhood was in the friendship of friends

The childhood was in the mischiefs and mistakes.

The childhood was in the flying on the horizon

Childhood, childhood, childhood, childhood

Every day, new dreams were created with cousins

The childhood of mine

The childhood of small cousins

Every Child Has Childhood and memories

The childhood of the house is still alive in my heart

Childhood, childhood, childhood, childhood

LOVE STORY

How much pain is hidden in my life,

Know how terrible is my love story.

I have seen everything in my youth,

There is no need to know anything gory.

How grateful whenever I smile

How much I am infamous at my territory.

I am always happy to make other's laugh,

I am hiding in the excuses for laughing glory.

There are so many things to hide in this life,

I am afraid to tell the whole thing, everybody.

How much fun it is to make other, own,

There is always remain shortage of effort to please own's dearie.

Suddenly, in my eyes,

Pain has found me in everybody's arbitrariness flory.

HEART BROKEN

Heartbroken a lot I am, heart like to burn the world,

What are you gonna tell me about your trust?

heartbeat asked me what has happened to me,

let me just say that this pain I got from you.

Dreams are all broken, now it is only heart left,

Break it also, it is time to an end.

The mistake is not the only mine, but also you are mistaken too,

Don't you know, what happened to me?

Life has also been dull, the calmness has also gone.

Still, I am ready for you today. Come join me with my heart,

If you will say yes, then I will show you everything again.

Heart-broken a lot I am, heart like to burn the world.

LOVE

Love makes the human go nimble

Love makes human heart tingle

Love creates pressure within the neurons

Love creates a vacuum in single

Love makes both weaknesses and strengths

Love makes your life simple

Love makes a man and woman bond.

Love is loved by loving individuals.

Love creates both havoc and peace

Love makes lips sing its jingle.

ILLUSION PART 1

I am the only one, living at this time.

I was surrounded by the thought of slime,

I had the feelings, but

No love, no peace, no hatred and no crime.

Then, when she came,

my feelings change.

The heart was thumping,

And that was very strange.

She was standing at my door,

Knocking it like firing aim,

may she was waiting for me,

And was calling my name.

I rushed to the door,

for opening the lock.

She was looking pretty,

and I was in shock.

After seeing me like this,

Her smile was getting wide.

After entering in,

She was looking so pride.

ILLUSION PART 2

She holds my hand,

And came closer,

gave a kiss on my cheek,

Filled with love, affection and pleasure.

She was still standing close to me

I held her from her waist

And I bent forward

To kiss her glowing face.

Her lips were close to mine,

Her deep black eyes were looking straight in mine,

The beautiful moment was a second far,

and suddenly everything shines.

LOVER

The reason for my love is definitely you,

I love the way you are, I love what you do.

you are such a cute lady with your ultimate style,

your care and love make me worthwhile.

you are my best buddy and my lover too

you are my life and I love you...

You are my boss, you are my girl

You are so lovely, you are my pearl

You are the best thing happened to me

you are my reason to be happy and glee

You are a lover, you are a giver

I am nothing without her

You are my partner in crime

You are my sunshine

I was lost you found me

I was loose you bound me

I was dying you save me

How can I thank you

you fill colours in my B/W life

you completes me with your love

Don't leave for god sake

Only love we can bake

You are my life and I love you...

YOU GIRL

I met her on my friend's place

She is elegant with all grace

Her smile her style so different

Add on her attitude first place

Dark eyes pink lips sharp features

Look like my high school teachers

She is like ocean's pearl

That curly haired girl

She is a cute girl

Though she is my ex

Respect her for all her decisions

For me or the next

She is elder in the age

That was only outrage

Now she is happy in her life

And now I have my own wife.

DRIZZLING CAME IN THE COURTYARD OF NATURE

Drizzling came in the courtyard of nature.

How much beauty was brought in its small bright body?

Clouds sang much-needed music.

This lush evening made us frantic.

Dry rivers again found beautiful New Life,

Look at the dancing beauty of a short wave.

How many new plants have sprouted in the forest park?

Bring the yellow flower and greenery again.

Peacock in the forest dancing and swans are enjoying.

new clouds are seeing their image.

every moment we play and dance in the rain,

and make our world and life delicious.

In your small home, lives the world of happiness.

Grishma Singh

Grishma Singh is pursuing B.Sc in Media science. She is a resident of Kolkata . Her hobbies include singing and dancing along with holding a formal training in these for 5 years and 3 years respectively. She recently discovered her love for writing which allowed her to pen down her thoughts smoothly and efficiently. Being born in an art-rich city , writing comes very naturally to her . She believes she's a learner and she's learning this art form. She is determined and would strive to do better , paving a way for scope of improvement.

You can contact her through email -
grishmasingh.bd@gmail.com

OPEN LETTERS

How I Met You

Dear Sourav,

It's not much of a time when you entered into my existent small world of remarkable confusions where I didn't know whether things were tangled or I am supposed to detangle pretty much present messed-up stuffs . I'm a social butterfly but at the same time I'm not (on Facebook). I still remember that fine evening when my notification showed : "Sourav Chatterjee sent you a friend request" My utter curiosity to go through a profile of all my confusions buster was ready to stalk this ethereal being . "Oh well, he's from our college, let's accept" As talks flourished I came to know a literary star , along with being a topper ,photographer and what not!. "Should I send him a song sang by me?" a question remained.

Keeping all these questions aside, I sent my voice note . "You sing great!" he replied. "Yeah, you get added into my fan list". There a lovely conversation begins to strike. Exchanging phone numbers for the sake of internship is where our friendship journey began. A Media student thought I need to make use of this opportunity to attain the best for future, a friend thought at least someone cares about a media student's future!. Along with works , I came to know a human being who can read someone like a book, understand someone like a friend , help someone like a guide. As the friendship, nah! a brother-sister relationship(now) developed I came across a remarkable personality who'll never judge you for your mindless questions and will never question your stupidity. A boy who keeps a girl's dignity at the foremost position, a boy who ceases at words while explaining how much you matter to him, but finds you his responsibility at least for the time you're with him, will give you enough reasons to laugh.

Silently wishing the best for you, never hoping a single tear drop to fall from your eyes. That kind of amazing you're! To me you became a mentor with whom I'd like to venture into this vast arena of media, you're like a solution for a girl whose perplexed thoughts seem to have an unfixed end . Lastly I would like to describe you in two lines:

"If anybody got the power to control sand's direction drifted by wind,

That would be you, for you're one of a kind..."

Yours' truly,

Grishma

LOVER- A LONG DISTANCE RELATIONSHIP

Dear Love,

"Your way of talking gives me a glimpse of you belonging to Delhi, do you?"

"I don't", I replied.

I still get back to that winter night when this message popped up on my messenger. Previously, I was stuck in the hassle of life. Not knowing what life actually stands for. My life was without an aim just like a ship without a rudder. The innocence and jolly nature which people tried to extract for their betterment became the foremost reason for you to admire me, adore me. "Hey I recently met a guy online, he enjoys my lame jokes as dank is too mainstream for him ! Might be that he's faking a laughter but doesn't he sound amazing?" I messaged my best friend. My best friend wasn't sure about what I was up to. He told me not to fall in trap of "online world", but who cares I am going to widen my limitations. I stayed firm on my decision to carry on with our longer conversations. Flashbacks tell how you transformed a soul filled with romanticism to a girl "never mind, you can compliment me some other Day". I remember how badly I wanted my Bollywood aims to be fulfilled, featuring a hero proposing me by lying down on his knees , sadly it went out like me proposing you , not lying on the knees but lying on the bed with a phone in my hand , talking to you via headset . The proposal day started with a threat from my best friend : If you don't propose him today, don't message me from tomorrow. These words of utmost fear accelerated my actions but with a deep-rooted pain of my Bollywood aims remaining unfulfilled forever. That evening I was having a chit chat with my friends, you called, my over exaggerated expressive behaviour accepted that I missed you , the sigh of relief was your reply : I was missing you too. Inner instinct whispered: It is good to know that I'm not suffering alone! I gathered my senses and came back to the conversation , "umm, be online at night , my friends are suspecting me about some unlawful work as I'm talking to you by coming away from them." Meanwhile I realised, that stupid smile across my face while talking was making them suspicious. My habit of giving surprises to make people happy allowed me to execute the proposal over video call. I was shook by the way how you always find me looking like a poop over video calls but never cease to smile when I laugh my heart out. My gloomy smile and undefined talks made me realise how bad I'm at proposing , it was indeed a disgustingly failed idea. "Can we switch over voice call" your lips murmured,the words of wisdom! You don't know how much thankful I'm to you for understanding how disgusting I'm at telling my feelings face to face. 23rd February , 2:30 am : "Grishma do you like me? Inner me: he's asking as if doesn't ! Why are boys so rude ! You can propose ! I'm not going to eat you up! On the outer I was the sweetest of the honey you've ever tasted. "Yes I do, like it's not love but I like talking to you". I know it was a proposal full of excuses, just to preserve my badge of honor of being a girl, girls deserve proposals, they don't propose themselves. I was astonished by the way how you showcased your feelings by quoting me as one the most important persons in your life and how you don't want to lose me for the reason "distance". Being proud about my expressive personality was reduced to ashes when I came across such a flawless proposal from an introvert's side. I remember how the idea of "an ideal romantic date" never existed for one year even if your eyes searched me in your hardest of the times, our dates were dark nights , late night conversations drinking the painful times even if deep down we knew it was a momentary happiness rejuvenating our tired souls. Our first meeting, our first union made a girl grow, a little bit more from inside, she got matured, handling everything on her own. I saw you at the airport, how I ran at highest of my running speed to jump upon you and hug with all of my efforts, when you came up with a remark : you're not that short as I thought, there's no use of heeled soles now. I hit you with a smile but from inside I made sure you don't get hurt. I felt your hands gushing through mine, I was living a dream with open eyes. We made it possible, we are going to make everything fall in place if we keep holding hands like this. Our meeting was a satisfaction without any regrets. Three days went like three hours but we lived our lives like it's today or never. The day you were supposed to return, my heart sank a little."How much time I again need to wait to see you again?" I tried holding my tears, tried holding your hands with best of my power but was immensely weak in front of the tides of time. "5 minutes left, I need to go"; my slow pale voice whispered. I was hugging you tight, with best of my efforts but feared what if I grow weak, what if I cry, I rushed to leave that place as soon as possible. I turned around, just to see you smiling at me. I lost control upon my feelings, I cried, I again ran, again turned ,you were there waving a goodbye from the train gate . My inner instinct realised I'm a loser in holding my feelings, waving you a goodbye with tears in my eyes whereas you were so strong to maintain that painful smile upon your face. While I was returning, your call to check upon me made me feel a bit alright until the time you uttered : "heels isn't going to add an extra inch to a short girl like you" your trial to make me laugh worked and I again started smiling even if I was unsure about whether our stars are destined to bless us or not. It's been one and half years I've been with you and nothing has changed. You still find me a weird looking creature whose hairs are never going to get fixed. We've made thousands of songs together, ruining every other song we got hold of. You ate more, and I got fat. We're maybe inversely proportional but rightly aligned with each other . Here you see, I'm bad with flirting as well. But still you accepted me with my every flaw. I know I've been adamant at times, complaining about silliest reasons, you regarding them as "petty" and me hopping upon you with thousands of questions which are still unanswered. It's amusing to find a companion like you, who dances as bad as me but have a dream of a flawless couple dance. I feel amazed whenever I think about how you never addressed me by "My Princess" but definitely the doll "Anabelle"; even though your eyes fills with glitters whenever you see me smiling . The feelings sown into deep of my heart requires you, it was looking for you yesterday, it still needs you and would need you ever after. I'm trying hard to be with you , hitting efforts with double of its intensity and I'll fight till the day I find myself successful. You and me are meant to be together and I'll prove that since some promises are meant to be kept forever.

Yours' lovingly,

Grishma.

J.Naresh Kumar

J Naresh kumar resides in Hyderabad and is a well known hotelier. After completion of Bachelor's degree in Science, he chose to enter into hotel management and is presently enjoying his Profession as a chef who
is excellently skilled in making European and Indian cuisines. His hobbies are writing, reading novels, and loves to innovate tasty food in his kitchen.

Emil: j.naresh2498@gmail.com

Instagram: @chef_n_salt

OPEN LETTER

My Love,

The words which are coming from my heart are the feelings that I expect from you. If you don't react to my love the way I expect you should, then my feelings would drown into an ocean, like the waves having no direction. My feelings for you would then turn into a cyclone that will harm me endlessly.

The purpose of love that I am giving you won't be fulfilled if it doesn't satisfy the emotions that bring agony to our hearts. If the expectations from each other aren't understood well it will definitely affect our relationship and our love and affection for each other might get disturbed.

Reaching our destination of love isn't difficult if our hearts smile with happiness and shed tears with pain. All these good and bad memories will make our bond stronger and beautiful.

Yours Forever,

Naresh

Navreet Kaur

Navreet is currently pursuing her Bachelors of Technology from New Delhi, India. She believes that every human has a story and every story deserves to be told. The biggest fan of coffee, skylines, rainy days and sunsets, she believes that travel is the way to lose yourself, yet be found. Reading and writing aren't just hobbies, but a way of life for her. Her key interests include public speaking, social work and leadership. She is trying to create her version of 'impact', one day at a time.

ELEMENTS OF LIFE

I am the elixir: cool, serene and calm,

I am the element known to cause the least harm.

I quench your thirst with my moist love,

With springs from below, and rains from above.

Who will you complain to if I withdraw my drops,

With your red, burnt faces and parched crops?

Your plants will have no strength, your beasts no force,

Your land will be barren and life so coarse.

I am water,

Earth's so called calmest daughter.

The sun, vehement heat reflects,

An orb of burning, a fiery aspect.

You need my heat, you need my fire,

Yet strive to avoid my wrath and ire.

I can burn and I can scorch,

I can light and I can torch.

And in a moment, the world I will consume,

And all therein, in that great day of doom.

I am fire,

Beware of my consuming ire.

I suppose I'm the one you can't control,

I am the breath of your living soul.

I ask the man who's near his death,

What wouldn't he do for one last breath?

The desperate, breathless man who craves supply,

The fowls, beasts and all mortals shall die.

Since you're leaving me devastated and spent,

Bid adieu to your dear element.

I am air,

You're losing my care.

Among my sisters, I count not myself the least,

I am the mother of all man and beast.

I am the reason for all soil and green yield,

I am the harbour of orchard, garden and field.

I rest your cities upon my mighty chest,

I am the mother that holds your nest.

I'll say no more but this I add must,

Remember human, your build is of my dust.

I am land,

In your life, I have the biggest hand.

I am the Earth, these are my daughters,

My land and air, fire and waters.

In my lap, my daughters intertwine,

And on my bosom, life doth shine.

Mankind, ay, long before your birth,

Alluring was the beauty of the Earth.

Then I bore the weight of pollution on my chest,

Which stabbed me hard, my daughters wrest.

Mind this, I'm not yours, you cheats,

I am for the future generations to keep!

Remember whether you're buried or burned,

You are the Earth, and to the Earth you'll return…

A WALTZ WITH SORROW

This lass, the one I scribe about,

I saw her first on a dreary night out.

She sat on the sidewalk, as the heavens poured,

In a night so forlorn, her eyes explored.

Her eyes of amber, with a glint so striking,

She turned to me, her gaze so spiking.

In that moment, my eyes fell on a gash,

I inched towards her, fearing an outlash.

Her eyes met mine as I closed the distance,

I stopped mid-way, watched her grow tense.

Unexpectedly, a broken, weak smile appeared,

Followed by a quivering lip and endless tears.

Scrawny her frame, and waddly her walk,

"Who are you, fair lady?", I talk.

"Why does it matter so much?", she exclaimed,

"I'm the face of ugly circumstance, we don't get named".

I stepped back at that poignant response,

Took some time to re-adjust my stance.

Her eyes still gushing as much as the skies above,

Lightning uniting with thunder, like people in love.

I asked again, "What's your story, fair lady?"

She smiled at me, her expression so shady.

She stepped towards me, with her hand outstretched,

Her words in my memory, will stay forever etched.

I took her hand, and sat as she narrated,

The chronicle of tribulation, her mind collated.

"I am you, and you are me,

You are a sapien, and I, your misery.

I make you feel, I make you sense,

I make you jump over the fence".

She stalls for a moment, clutches my finger,

It's deja vu from heartbreak trying to linger.

"You adore my friend, her name's Glee,

Has she ever made you feel as much as me?

I know what's strength, I know how to stay,

I can show you intensity in a magnificent way.

She is your ally since she brings along a smile,

But tears and frowns - they go a longer mile.

I am here to cure you of your addiction,

Ever-lasting happiness is only a product of fiction".

"Love me too, for I can't stay till eternity,

I will only come back in trials of betrayal and infirmity.

If I wouldn't be your esteemed associate,

You would never, happiness appreciate".

She rose mid-sentence, started to walk away,

I reached out to stop her from parting this way.

My fingers circled her, but my hands couldn't grip,

I looked everywhere, couldn't see her as she slipped.

The heavens boomed, the rain fell furiously,

I looked at the steely, tempestuous skies rather curiously.

I heard articulation, so strained my ear in attention,

"I am sorrow", the voice did mention.

A human so petty, I stood rather humbled,

In the face of dolefulness, my strength had crumbled.

A meek "Thank you!", I'd sounded,

In a realisation so colossal, I stood binded.

"Sorrow is but knowledge, a quest,

Those who know mourn the deepest."

AGAINST THEIR 'BETTER JUDGEMENT'

They speak of crime and sin,

Of ethics and conscience,

Of white robes and orange cholas,

Fables of doings and misdoings.

They speak of Hindus and Muslims,

Sikhs, Christians, Buddhists, Jews,

Of theism and skepticism,

Debate on religion and spirituality.

They speak of caste and creed, race and clan,

Of being 'straight' or 'not-so-straight',

Of being a man or the 'lesser gender',

Conjecture on one's identity.

They speak of human frame:

Tall and lanky or short and stout?

Big eyes or a roman nose?

Judgement on things beyond one's control.

They speak of abilities,

Science and math, or plain old art and drama?

But, can she cook and clean? But, does he earn?

Disregard for personality types as a whole.

They speak of choices,

Of singlehood or marriage,

Of parenting a child, or a pet,

Alternatives which they never really alternate.

— —

They speak, and we listen.

They command, and we obey.

They decree, and we never dismantle it.

Notions we never really question.

We are 'they', every one of us,

Living in our own society's prohibitions.

With mandates and regulations,

Forbidding us from being ourselves.

It's time we learn a lesson:

Of tolerance and acceptance,

Of respect and consideration.

Learn to live. And let others live!

TOXIC TOUCH: POETRY ON CHILDHOOD SEXUAL ABUSE

His eyes,

Lust shining through them,

Like innocence shone through hers.

His hands,

Rough and calloused in places,

The contrast so stark,

Against the softness,

Of her baby skin.

His presence,

Tall and looming,

Against her short frame,

Almost symbolic,

Of his physical advantage.

His smile,

So shrewd, so smirky,

Against hers,

Which started and ended in innocence.

The tender age of 9,

And a fragile understanding,

Or should I say un-understanding,

Of the wicked world around?

Sensations of pleasure,

Making waves through his body,

Feelings of terror,

Of morbid denial,

Making waves through hers.

A 30 year old,

Using a 9 year old,

With no mercy, no regrets,

Grinding and moving against flesh untouched.

Why couldn't he understand,

That a body,

Can be washed,

Stripped of all sin and crime.

But a mind, a heart

A conscience, a soul,

Lost itself,

Unwillingly.

This is but rape,

Brutal and heart-wrenching,

For touch can be toxic,

But its memories?

Fatal.

OPEN LETTERS

Things I Couldn't Say To My Bully:

An Open Letter to All The 'Cool' Kids

Dear 'cool kids',

We are the nerds. Nameless faces. Dissociative identities. The visages lined with stress lines, which escape every eye in caterwauling classrooms. The ones who plop down near a secluded window and surrender to a world which feels more real than the one we reside in. People who would rather have an all- consuming love affair or a fleeting summer romance with fictitious personalities, and would choose the fragrance of an old hardcover falling apart at the seams over any synthetic perfumes.

We feel in alphabets and cry in quotes, we are souls fluent in the language of emotion. We are the people who would choose a winter afternoon in bed, with coffee and a book over a Saturday night at exclusive pubs, drunk and high on adrenaline. We get high too. We get high on books. They would call us names - nerd, bookworm, geek, low-life being the classic insults.

They're music to our ears now. That's how strongly we're accustomed to being called names. And yes, we got called them all. We'll never know why it's scarcely understandable to some that this is how we derive pleasure. This is how we create relief. This is how we function, survive, get through our lives and those long drawn days and nights of being picked on and being made to feel for choices we made for ourselves. We get hurt, we cry too. We feel trodden upon too, we feel let down too. Because sometimes we hide in book aisles and libraries, book stalls and archives because it's a world where we're sure of not being hurt anymore. At least not until we choose that genre. Given the option, we'd still be ourselves. Because we may be boring and low life, but our books? They will always be interesting and high up on the radar. To all the 'cool' people out there – we'd never be you.

We'd never need to.

Yours,

Navreet Kaur.

AN UPHILL CLIMB:

An Open Letter To Those Who Wish To Give Up

Dear fellow strugglers,

It's precision and perfection, perseverance and perception,

That bring one to success. It's dedication and determination, discipline and decidedness. That help one to attain success. It's virtues and values, collaboration and cooperation, that help one to retain success.

The greatest battles in the history of mankind are always psychological and are always fought from within. One takes on tough targets, pushes to the limit, surpasses all expectations and emerges triumphant - all as a consequence of one conscious decision. The conscious decision to never give up when that little voice inside of us tells us to rest our tools. That little voice must always be answered by the steady dignity that refuses to give in, the courage that keeps one going. Every moment is an opportunity. All that is required to transform that opportunity to experience is focusing on what's important, capturing time and doing away with negativity. If things don't work out, take a moment to review, revise and redo, everything will gradually fall into place. If there was ever an analysis of one trait common to all successful people, it would be a do-or-die attitude. We all have our moments of weakness, we all have times when we want to sit back and relax, but they say, if you trudge through at that point, you'll make it to your destination. Weakness is a human trait, but a never- say-die spirit is the mark of a man who is (or is soon to

be) successful.

So what must we do now? Step up, empower ourselves to climb to the zenith of our potentials, because each one of us is a success story waiting to unfold.

Yours,

Navreet Kaur.

Romila Chitturi

72

Romila is an awards-winning writer and author of 6 published ebooks. A friendly, helpful and a happy person. She loves good food, road trips, coffee, fashion, poetry and lots of music. She has been with paper and pen since she was a teenager. She started blogging in 2004 to continue her passion for writing that she always held, allowing her to be creative in her own little space on the internet, and hopefully to inspire, relate to people and maybe even make them think, feel and sometimes laugh with her words.

FAITH

Faith is confidence

Faith is assurance

Faith is humbling oneself, before the unknowable

Faith is respecting our comprehensive limits in a limitless world.

Faith is stepping outside the boundaries of logic without having to take a huge leap

Faith is giving light to darkness

Faith is touching and filling the void

Faith is prayer

Faith is hope

Faith is God

Faith is someone will do for me what I am willing to do for them

Faith is that people in my life to know they can count on me

Faith is if they fall ,I will pick them up. If they can't walk, I will carry them.

faith is belief in something without evidence

Faith is a psychological help in times of crisis

Faith is a virtue with positive connotations.

Faith is the thing that helps me to see that through difficulties

Faith is the human race which expects the best out of everyone in our lives.

KINDNESS

Showing a little kindness, a little compassion can go such a long way

Everyone can be kind, it is a suit that everyone can wear

Kindness sticks with you, it's when you see that someone is struggling,

With so much negativity in the world, we all need more positivity,

I treat people the way I would want to be treated

Treat people with empathy and it opens so many doors,

You never know what could happen

The power of kindness is infectious.

Do what makes you happy,

Fill your time with things you enjoy and love.

At the end of the day this is your life

Never forget the importance of your own happiness.

Don't let anything jeopardise it,

Kindness attracts kindness.

It is one of those things that doesn't even take much to do,

It is something that everyone seems to overlook sometimes.

BOOKS

We take books for granted but why?

The fact is they have become a part of human life, from childhood to old age

Can we name anything other than books that may be so justly called the quintessence of

the human mind?

Our mind is receptive to ideas, knowledge and wisdom which the books provide in

abundance.

An idea from a book is ample food for thought for a lifetime

Books are essential for intellectual sustenance

Books influence minds of men radically

Books have the power to delight and enthral the human minds endlessly

Books serve as a social correctives

Books are reformers in revolutionising public opinion

Books are inseparable from human life

Books are the ideal companions in solitude

Books are a source of inspiration, pleasure and mental contentment.

The influence of books on the human mind cannot be gainsaid

whether for the good and for the bad.

As we are unique creatures because of our intellectual faculties and they are expressed best in books.

AM I LOVEABLE?

My teeth aren't perfectly straight but they are pearly white.

To me, when I smile and it reaches your eyes

It's as though you really see me

I offer a little parcel of my heart.

I just can't stop loving

I always return to wanting to share love in my life.

I manage to express how I feel and who I am in so many wondrous ways,

I watch myself transform into the young girl

Filled with laughter, teasing and silliness.

Every day I learn something new.

I get excited when the challenge ahead seems a little daunting.

I use my body to feel the world around me

I love to enjoy the small pleasures of each day;

I express my soul and what I hold in my heart through my words, actions and energy.

It gives me joy to see me on fire with my passion for living and being myself.

My laughter is infectious and lifts the mood of those around me,

I love seeing the humor in the beautiful ridiculousness of life

Do I feel loveable? Yes I do.

MY LOVE AFFAIR WITH WORDS

I am a writer and I love words.

I love telling stories, stories of life, stories of humans, stories of emotions

I feel a sense of wholeness when I write.

I hold a pen and start writing in a notebook

I write to understand my reactions to different situations.

I write to make sense of how others react to me.

I write so that I can feel one with my thoughts.

I write to express thoughts in my head, to bring out parts of myself into something tangible

Writing expresses feelings in a way that is only possible through the process of putting words on paper–and that is an irreplaceable experience.

Writing is a soothing exercise which helps me to make sense of the world by exploring my own written ones.

I can access the minds of the readers and touch their lives with my words. My Love for words has no reason.

Writing allows me space and time to express myself more authentically than I might in conversations.

LOVE NEEDS AN OPEN HEART

The Best thing in life is love – to be loved, to love and be loveable.

Yet, is there anything more complex and abstract than love?

You don't get it when you need it most but you open pay heavily for it.

Still we hunger for more love every moment of our life.

Love is the most burning and perishable of all human passions.

It sometimes inflicts the most festering wound within us when its labour is lost.

It can sting like a hornet or stab like a knife.

Love has the least amount of pity. In love, even the nicest things count.

When we open our hearts to our fellow human beings, we start giving and receiving love.

Love can flourish only in the field of human relationship.

Love is a well from which we can drink only as much as we have put in, and the stars that

shine from it are only our eyes looking in it.

People who do not chose to act in love, who deny love to others out of fear or loss, their

lives in barren and empty.

The strings of love are like the strings of a violin.

Once you have learned the rules you must play with your heart.

It then requires no map or chart.

You only need an open heart.

I LOVE YOU

We have come so far so right

That we have no left to go

Read my couplets, they are stars which twinkle

They say "I love you", so you know

You know I can't draw pictures

Or sing songs

But I can hold you tight in your sleep

And fly you to starry bright night to the moon

Because I am not there as a person

Doesn't mean I'm not with you

All these pieces of papers with

Thousands of words

For you, is the proof how much I love you

I don't like your sad memories, I am here to make you laugh

The happy memories which we make will never make you cry

Holding hands and watching movies

Here is the best start of our lives

Everything says ' I love you' so you know it right.

THE LAST DAY

Live life as if there was no tomorrow.

Live each moment as if it were your last.

We all have decided what our future is going to be like.

We all have thought over where we see ourselves ten years down the line

But what if today is my last day as alive?

I would fulfil my fantasies. I do not wish to attach morals with this thing.

Seeking pleasure is not wrong after all. It is important to feel good within, literally!

I would explore my inner realms.

I would just let my insides rip me apart and get printed on a piece of paper.

Emerge as a super power on my last day. Give justice. Or just be a death breathing avenger.

Feel happy. Love myself.

Embrace that mirror and go, splurge!

Food, for me, can no longer be related to survival, indulge into a blissful moment of epiphany. And when cheese is here, how can I forget the irresistible wine?

I would love to pamper myself hard and give myself an enigmatic royal treatment.

Make an indulgence out of the basics. Binge in!

HEARTFELT

We're all always thinking about love even when we don't call it by its name.

We think about the love that we've had and won and that we've lost.

We think about the love that could have been and would have been and never meant to be.

Some say that joy and happiness are the fruits of love.

Some determine that love cannot exist without pain.

My love is a confession of my character, let the people who I love tell the world who I am.

My love is in which you confess that you are hopeful, beautiful, sacrificial and exceptional and always a little bit or a lot, afraid

But still always ready to let love be spectacular – risks considered, foolishness felt, rarity endured. If we do this, how can we not love better?

And even if and when those people cannot return that love in the same way, let it speak of the beauty and the resilience of my soul.

Love is the most spectacular thing about my life.

Love is the sun that shines brightly throughout my day.

Love is the gravity that holds me down in every way.

Love is the moon that shimmers through my night.

Love is the star that glimmers oh so bright.

The 'heartfelt' love defines me!

THE INTERNET

I email. I search. I shop. I Tweet. I stream. I Duo.

Stroke by stroke, as I slip deeper into the Internet's embrace,

I find myself wondering: "What if the Internet went away for a day?"

Text, e- mail, twitter, Instagram, Facebook, who are we really without that little red

notifications?

How lost we'd be without Google Maps?

How lonely we'd feel without access to music and podcasts?

"Send me a pic," long distance crush asked me on my last phone date

"Okay," I blush. Then I panic. How?

A day without internet grab a book, take a nice open corner by the window

prepare a mug full of coffee and read to the fullest.

Internet the biggest distraction that doesn't let us relax for even a minute

Put on those shoes, take the pet along, or call friends and go walking.

Who knows nature might amaze like never before.

Life today would be difficult without internet, to say the least.

But unplugging isn't the worst thing in the world.

I believe by the saying "life moves pretty fast. If you don't stop and look around once in a

while, you might miss it."

Suchismita Ghosal

Hailing from a small city Malda, West Bengal, Suchismita dreams high to touch the sky. She is an avid reader, writer, poet, muser, scribbler, storyteller, published author, blogger, nature lover, social worker & a freelance model. She will soon complete her graduation in Zoology.

She has also completed her advanced diploma in Computer Application. She has authored more than 100 anthologies as a co-author, most of them are in process of publication. Her debut book titled "Fields of Sonnet" will soon be launched.

She is also a columnist of "The post India" digital news website, "Youth Ki Awaaz" digital media website, & "Obaa" by Girltable community. Her articles have been published on "Digital eNews", an australian digital newspaper ," The Good Men Project" , a renowned american digital news website & she is a verified member of "She Will Speak", an american women empowering organisation.

She is also a web content writer on various community like The Poet's Weed , Peholics , Buzzure Media Works, The Inked Square, Ink That Never fades, Fantasised, Inkophile & so on.

As a compiler & editor, she has compiled two books, "Unspoken Tales of a Hero" & "Eden of Memories", which are now available in online bookstores.

She aspires to become a great author & heal people through her words' majesty in the future. She is available on her instagram account @storytellersuchismita & her email id –

ghoshalsuchismita019@gmail.com

OPEN LETTERS

An Open Letter To My Brother Who Was Adopted

To my cute younger brother,

I don't know what it is that always makes me a little bit extra careful to you, but whenever I feel an urge to make you happy from the core of my heart, I feel blessed. I won't ask for your whereabouts as it was just yesterday we talked for hours over phone & felt a little bit pain of missing you more when heard you confessing that you're missing me too.

Hostel life is the toughest thing, I agree. Getting your all the work done by yourself, having no family members by your side, especially when you're physically ill, having your food on time & adjusting with 2 or 3 more unknown roommates are never an easy thing. You are on your 11th stooped with the pressure of dozens of heavy books , & more over residing alone in a new city leaving your own home thousand miles away might be a hardcore struggling things but the way you talk, proves how much you are strong & giving efforts to make yourself comforted! And, here I am, truly appreciating your hard work & my respect has been twice for you than the time you left your new school.

You were only a 4 years old child when mom & dad clutched your little fingers & took you to our home. It was my one of my biggest dreams to have a little brother like you which insisted them to turn my dream into reality & take you for us to live a better life together. I still remember the child you used to be ; a pair of beautiful voluptuous eyes, sweet smile & the purest heart that you used to make my heart smitten for you the moment I first saw you. Trust me, we never felt you're someone else, different from our sweet little family or someone outsider in our little world of happiness, rather you were, is & always will be the main source of happiness. From the day you entered in our home, our home got filled with full of beguiling smile, enlightenment & pious love.

Playing with you all the time, making you feed & bath by my own, having your demands fulfilled, sharing ice creams, chocolates, laugh, love, sorrow & tears together, having cat-fights & fun together & then spending a lot of golden memories together have been the most precious wealth for me. I've kept all our moments locked in the core of my heart. I know you've always made us proud & will keep on doing so. From scoring excellent in your studies to winning trophies in various fields of activities, you have always made us head held high for you. Undoubtedly the love you received from us have returned us with your innumerable success & smile. Sill in case, if you've ever felt bad by thinking yourself separated from us or, felt alone ,disappointing or valueless & hiding your problems with a pretence of smiling, I will say please never feel such or, bring such depressing thoughts in your mind, brother as we all love you more than anything & can't think ourselves separated from you. We miss you in our every blink. Mom & dad are continuously suffering from a deteriorating health & becoming diminutive in your absence. We all want to see you touching limits of sky & restlessly waiting for the vacation to see you soon. Our eyes are thirsty to catch a glimpse of you!

Remember, I'm always a call away in case you need me the most. Never feel demoralized or demeaned. Work hard, cross milestones & take care of your health always. Your sister will never stop loving you. Stay blessed & loved forever!

From,

Your own notorious sister.

AN OPEN LETTER TO THE YOUTH SLOWLY STRIVING TOWARDS THE DRUG ABUSE

To

The Youth Striving towards a Drug Addictive life,

Most of you are probably in the midst of your high school days or, have just stepped into the new college & are enjoying every bit of this. New life, new hope, new ecstasy & new peers, in a word, it might be "celestial" but the continuous peer pressure on taking drugs or smoking weeds should be the first & foremost thing to avoid.

This is really tough to just say 'No' when your friends insist saying , "It's common for men" or laugh out when you protest further. It might be the reason for low self-esteem or self-respect but gaining a healthy life will be the best choice to make. Drugs or any means of addiction can be dangerously lethal. I've faced all of it. From being an innocent fresher in my college who knows nothing about drugs to being the spoiled brat totally drowning myself in the abyss of excessive drug addiction, my life became the scariest nightmare ever losing track of my life's mainstream! The constant beckoning of those demonic tranquil days didn't leave any way for me to reject those urge of in taking drugs through injection, inhalation or ingestion. I wasn't even able to catch that I was slowly getting separated from my friends, family or any relation but kept on destroying my mind, brain & behaviour completely. It was too hard to control my emotions & urge to take doses more intensely day by day.

The effects of drug not only became the lifelong damage for me but also closed the door of return back into the mainstream almost. I stayed lying on the floor, turned 360° from the guy I used to be with my rapidly deteriorating health. It was my fate that my parents supported me when I was just about to be engulfed by death. They gambled all their money, drenched themselves with all their tears only in exchange of my priceless life. From admitting me to the most renowned rehabilitation hospitals to taking me to the doctors, they left no efforts undone & that only prayed for my life every moment. They didn't stop there, took care of me for sleepless days & nights, especially the moments I suffered from chronic excessive shiver, muscle cramps & dreadful asthma.

It might be looking like a long boring description to many of you who has already given their heart, soul & mind just for the 2minutes euphoric emotional pleasure or, floating in the utopian world but the damage it has started doing, can be fatal. It can be more dreadful when you will try to quit afterwards & face a dangerous withdrawal syndromes. Loss of appetite, increase of heart rate, blood pressure, frenzy blood vessels, heart attack, stroke, respiratory problems, psychosis, mental disease, PTSD, hepatitis even long term lethal diseases like AIDS (caused by repetitive use of same syringe) etc are the list of result for excessive drug abuse. Hope nobody would fall into such pernicious situations ever in their life.

It's good to leave the friendship that causes life, it's better to say 'no' to the fatal outcome & it's best to stay alone rather than the extreme repercussion snatches your parents' happiness. Try to understand the gravity & work for it. Choose a healthy life over anything, over any short term fatal pleasure. After all, life only gives a 2nd chance once!

From

The sufferer of drug addiction.